Allah

An introduction

Abdul Waheed

Allah (An introduction)

Abdul Waheed

PUBLISHED
AUTHOR
notionpress
.com
CERTIFICATE OF PUBLISHING
We're proud to present this certificate of publishing to
Abdul Waheed
for successfully publishing
ALLAH (AN INTRODUCTION)
on 24-01-2023
"A writer's life and work are not a gift to mankind; they're a necessity" ~ Toni Morrison

Dedication

This book is dedicated to the memory of my late father Haji Ubairdur Rahman (Munna) and younger brother Abdul Hameed. May God (Allah) give peace to his soul.

Aamen

Table of contents

Preface

In this book, a brief introduction has been given about Allah ie God. The extent of man is only subtle. It is not so easy to know and understand Allah, because man imagines on the basis of what he has got. How do you like this book? Please let me know if you have any more knowledge.

Thank you,
Date- 07/01/2023

Yours -- Abdul Waheed, Barabanki, UP, India.

Allah Introduction

(a) Essence - There is a very short surah in the Qur'an Majeed which is called Surah-e-Ikhlas. The meaning of its Arabic verses is as follows: 'O Prophet, say that He means Allah is One. Allah is baseless and omnipotent. He has no children, nor is he anyone's child, nor is anyone equal to him. Surah-e-Ikhlas is considered equal to one-third of the Qur'an Majeed. This is because the foundation of Muslim theology (Tawheed) has been laid on what has been said about Allah in this Surah. Oneness of Allah has been accepted in this Surah. Ax's summary is as follows: Allah is the only omnipotent being by whom the entire universe functions in an orderly fashion, and this is the cornerstone of Islam. Belief in Allah and all the rest of the beliefs and rules are the branches of this one root or tree. The source of everything that exists is Allah. We may or may not understand the truth of Allah, but there is no other option without accepting his existence. Allah is such a necessity. Without which we cannot solve the problems of the existence of the world. Allah is one and formless. Unity (Wahdat) means to be only one • Monotheism – It is the attribute of Allah that he is one in his form and one in his attributes. That is, Tawheed (monotheism) means to consider Allah as one or to believe in his oneness or to declare that he is one. Generally we can say that there is only God and there is no other God and this God is called Allah, then there is no part of this Allah.

He is One and Himself is One. There is nothing other than Allah and His attributes etc. The meaning of Adi is to be from forever and to remain forever. It should also be remembered that the thing which has no beginning means that it is said to be eternal from the beginning. The thing which has no end i.e. remains forever is called eternal. That's why Allah is eternal and eternal. When we can say that Allah is Aadi, it means that He is eternal or 'Wajibu Exist'.

Reasonable existence means that which does not exist with the support of others, that is, which is self-existent. It means a person who must exist and it is impossible for him not to exist. The one who will exist rationally will be Pranadi and will be eternal. It will neither have a beginning nor an end and it cannot be destroyed at any time. He himself will exist. That which is produced from another is brought into existence by the originator and cannot exist substantially. According to Islamic teachings, Allah is the only reasonable existence, apart from him, there is no reasonable existence. Allah is reasonable existence and it is necessary for reasonable existence to be complete in its own form. Therefore, all the qualities that are necessary for this perfection are fully present in Allah. These qualities are called Sifat Kamaliya. These properties will be discussed further.

Allah is omniscient, omniscient and omniscient. He has authority over everything. He is everyone's well wisher and food giver. He is the nurturer of all and the spoiler. He is running this earth from his Shradesh. He is the master and ruler of the world. Everything is subject to him. He is very kind. He is the forgiver of sins and the accepter of repentance. Allah has the quality of justice along with mercy.

In the light of the teachings of the Qur'an, only that entity is worthy of prayer and worship, who is formless, eternal, immortal, and eternal, who is forever and ever, who is omnipotent, master of all, omniscient, whose grace is all. be overshadowed; In whose knowledge and scholarship there is no fault; In whose justice there should be no doubt of treason; The one who gives life, who is the one who manages to maintain the fierce life; Who is the master of all the powers of profit and loss; Whose forgiveness, grace and care are all desirous of; To whom the whole world returns; The one who keeps everyone's account and who has the right to punish and reward. If we look at all the powers and things in the world, then we do not see any power or thing which is full of all these qualities. The Qur'an considers only one person to be a combination of all these qualities and that is Allah. He orders man to leave everything and put faith in Him. The meaning of the first part of the Kalima 'La-Ila-Il-Illa' is that there is no God other than Allah. This part of the Kalima has three pillars:

(a) Concept of one God (Unity). (b) The world and its things and nothing else is equal to it (this part is called Nafi or negative part).
(c) It is its own base (i.e. baseless) and all things are based on it. (i.e. it is half) (this fraction is called asbat or positive fraction).

Before we present any detailed description of Illami-beliefs regarding Allah, it seems necessary that whatever Muslim writers have expressed their views about Allah, we present them systematically here. Muslim students are taught a book titled :- 'Talim-ul-Islam'. This book has been written by Mufti Azam Muhammad Kafayat Ullah Sahib and in its second part a question is: 'What faith should Muslims have towards Khudatala? And his answers are as follows:

1 - Allah is one.

2- Allah alone is worthy of prayer and worship and none is worthy of worship except Him.

3 - He has no partner or partners. That is, there is no partner in the power of Allah, his attributes, his rights and ownership.

4 - He is omniscient. Nothing is hidden from him.

5 - He is omnipotent, omnipotent.

6- He has created the earth, sky, moon, sun, angels, humans, jinn means the whole world and he is its master. 7- Life and death are under his command. He kills and gives life. He is the provider of food for all the creatures of the world.

9- He himself neither eats nor drinks nor sleeps. 10 - He is eternal and eternal.

11 - No one gave birth to him.

12 -- He has neither father, nor son, nor daughter, nor wife, nor does he have any relative. He is free from all these bondages.

13 - All are dependent and based on him but he is baseless, he does not need anything.

14 - He is incomparable, nothing is equal to him 15 - He is free from all errors.

16 -- He has no shape - type. He has neither hands, nor feet, nor ears, nor nose.

17 – He has made the angels and appointed them for the management of the world and for special tasks.

18-He sent prophets to guide his creation to teach humans the true religion, to tell good things and to save them from bad things.

(b) **different names of Allah**

Many names of Allah have come in the Quran Majeed. 'Rab' is the most famous of these names. The original meaning of this word is nurturer. Then naturally many meanings have been added to it and thus this word has gained a lot of wideness. This word is used in three meanings in the Qur'an.

(i) The name 'Rab' is used in the sense of master or lord or master. That is, Allah is the Lord of the whole world and Lord of all the living beings. We can say that Rab is the master, master and master. This is a basic belief of Quran Majeed.

(ii) The second meaning of 'Rab' is the maintainer, the protector, the maintainer. (iii) The third meaning of 'Rab' is Hakim, Ruler and Administrator, Creator, Manager. It is worth remembering that the Qur'an lays more emphasis on Allah being 'Rab', while the Holy Scriptures teach that Allah is not only the Lord of this creation and creatures, but also the 'Abba' of human beings. There is also a father. Muslim scholars consider Allah to be the father of humans, 'Abba', an abominable idea and lay more emphasis on the mastery of Allah than the fatherhood of Allah.

The name 'Ar-Rahman' has also been presented for Allah in the Qur'an. The word is usually translated as one who is kind to. But if we scrutinize this word, it will be clearly visible that this word is made up of combination of Ghar and Rahman. The word 'Raman' or 'Rahmana' was prevalent among the Christian people of western Arabia for God. From the use of the word 'Ar Rahman' in Quran Majeed, it can be concluded that the 'Khuda' of Muslims means Allah and the God of Christians.

Rahman is actually the same person. Late Professor Prajmal Khan Sahab, who was Maulana Azad's personal secretary and had studied Quran Majeed deeply, was a follower of this idea. Many names of Allah are mentioned in the Qur'an and in the Hadiths. The number of names excluding the word 'Allah' is 96 and these are called 'Ismay Hasan' i.e. beautiful names. If we look at the list of these 66 names, we will come to know that some names reveal the Jalali Sifat (Terrible Attributes) of Allah and some names reveal His Jamali Sifat (Glorious Attributes). . Muslim scholars are of the opinion that Allah is the only name which is the essential name of God, i.e. this name is the symbol of his existence. The remaining 66 names reveal the qualities of Allah. In Surah 7: 180 of the Qur'an it is written as follows: 'Beautiful names (attributes) belong only to Allah, so call upon Him by those names only. The list of all the names of Allah is not given in the Qur'an. But commentators have prepared a list of these names with the help of hadiths. A legend is related to

Abuhuraira that Hazrat Muhammad said, 'Verily, God has 66 names, whoever recites those names will enter heaven'. A list of 16 names has been given in this hadith. If the word Allah is added to these 66 names, then there are a total of 100 names. Religious Muslims often hold a rosary in their hands which contains a specific number of beads and with the help of these beads they chant or recite the names of Allah. Among the beautiful names of Allah, these two names 'Ar-Rahman' and 'Ar-Rahim' are well known. Similarly, 'Al Muntakrim' meaning the avenger and 'Alkuwi' meaning the one with strength, are two well-known names of Isme Jamaliya i.e. Tejaswi.

(c) The Nature of Allah and His Attributes

(i) Meaning of Form and Attributes - Neither do we find any clear idea regarding the form of Allah in Kurman Majeed, nor have the commentators written anything clearly on this subject. The only thing that can be said about the form of Allah is that the knowledge of his form is impossible. That's why a person should not try to know his nature. Only this much knowledge is sufficient that Allah exists, but His form is beyond human understanding. Just as vision does not work in front of the sun, in the same way the intellect thinks about the essence of the reality of Allah, but does not try to know its fact, because it is beyond the intellect.

Muslim scholars have discussed a lot on the relationship between the element or form of Allah and the elemental adjectives or qualities. The question was whether Allah's attributes or Taaliv adjectives are eternal like Allah or not? Mu'tazila+ was of the opinion that the attributes of Allah or the essence like knowledge, life, power etc. are in the form of Allah and are part of that form. Al-Ash'ari was of the opinion that the attributes of Allah are derived from his form, although like Allah, he is certainly eternal. Neither can they be called in the form of Allah nor can they be called Tul only. Man's conscience cannot know this mystery. There is no other option other than man to just accept it. In Muslim philosophy, an istilah (i.e. definitional) term 'bil kaif' (i.e., without questioning how, why) has been used to express this idea, which means that there are some mysteries which the human conscience cannot understand. Can . Man should accept those mysteries as they are. 2 Take only one attribute of Allah 'Word'. Allah sent Hazrat Musa

And talked to Hazrat Mohammad. Is this promise an eternal quality whose manifestation took place in the bondage of space and time? If the Qur'an is the word of Allah, is it created or is it uncreated? Motjila's opinion was that Karman was composed. The Mu'tazilah school of thought holds that Allah only planted thoughts in the mind of Muhammad, therefore the Qur'an is created and can be freely exchanged. But orthodox scholars do not agree with this view. They think that the Qur'an is eternal or uncreated, because the word of Allah is the eternal quality of Allah. This quality is outside the element or form of Allah (Outside of His Essence). From this brief discussion it is concluded that whatever is in the Qur'an should be accepted without questioning 'bil kaif' i.e. how and why. 'Love' is also an attribute of Allah. Undoubtedly Allah loves humans, but this love only means that He beautifies humans with all kinds of gifts, blessings etc., fulfills all their needs. In all this charity, Allah does not give himself for man (He does not give himself). This is the fundamental difference. Which is found in Islam and Christianity. This is the reason why the belief of sacrifice is invalid for Islam.

Although Allah reveals His goals, His thoughts and His will to man through revelation, He Himself is ideal and beyond reason. ,

+ That group of scholars who are supporters of independent ideology. The group of scholars who were of conservative ideology. Al-Amri was born in 7 AD and it was his view that faith is superior to reason.

We cannot call Allah a person in Islam, because the word 'person' comes only for human beings. Yet Allah is a personal God (Purusha). His personality is unique and unborn.

(ii) Seven special qualities - Muslim scholars have specifically mentioned seven qualities of Allah. These qualities are important and it is necessary to believe in these qualities like the existence and oneness of Allah. These properties are as follows:

Hayat (life)

Allah is alive and He alone is worthy of worship. He has no companion or partner. There is no fault or defect in his appearance. No one gave birth to him, nor does he give birth to anyone, he is invisible. It has no shape, form or colour. It can neither be cut nor divided. There is neither beginning nor end to his existence. He is immutable. If he wants, he can destroy the whole creation in a moment and if he wants, he can create it again in a moment. All this is not impossible for him. It is the same for him to create a fly and to create the seven heavens. Whatever happens, he has neither any gain nor any loss. If the infidel believes in him and becomes a follower of the rule of abstinence, then there is no benefit to him. Similarly, if all the believers become disbelievers, then there is no harm to him.

ilm (knowledge)

Knowledge means knowing. That is, Allah has knowledge of light and all things on earth. From his knowledge, no matter whether it is small or big, is not outside. He has knowledge of every particle. He knows everything before its beginning and also after its end. The thoughts that come in the heart of man are in the knowledge of Allah. Ilme Gab (Knowledge of the secret, indirect knowledge) is the special quality of Allah. His knowledge is eternal. He is free from mistake and error.

Nature

Strength means strength, that is, Allah has the ability to create the world, to keep it stable and to destroy and bring it into existence again. It is capable of taking a person from east to west and from west to east or the seventh Shrasman in a moment. His power is eternal and infinite.

intention

Intention means to act with one's authority. Allah brings into existence whatever He wills by His authority and destroys whomever He wishes by His authority. All the things in the world are under his authority and come into existence by his will. He is not compelled to do any work. Everything good and bad in this world is due to his will and whatever we do is due to his will. If someone asks why Allah doesn't make all human beings honest, then it is answered that all his actions and resolutions are beyond the understanding of man, he can do whatever he wants. He is voluntary, independent. This quality of Allah is also eternal.

samaa (hearing)

Sama means 'to hear'. Although Allah does not have ears like creatures, yet He hears everything. He hears the slightest sound. There is no difference between nearness and distance in front of him.

Basar (see)

Basar means 'to see'. All things are in the sight of Allah. But he doesn't have eyes like other animals. Just as there is no shape or form of his ears, in the same way there is no shape or form of his ankles. He sees the smallest thing and does not become a hindrance in his seeing. In the dark, a black ant walking on a black stone is not visible to him.

kalam (words)

Kalam means 'talking'. This quality of Allah is also eternal and perfect. He does not have a tongue like the creatures, nor is he dependent on the tongue for speech. He spoke to Musa and he spoke to Hazrat Muhammad in Shab-i-M'raj+. He communicates with people through the angel Gabriel and especially enlightens the prophets with his resolution. Quran is the word of Allah, eternal and corrupt, cursed.

(iii) Human qualities - Some such qualities of Allah are also mentioned in Quran Majeed. For whom it is necessary to have a body. Often these are the qualities which are found only in embodied beings.

+Shabe Ma'raj - It is narrated that one night Hazrat Muhammad was apparently taken to the seventh plane sitting on the back of a white horse where he saw Allah. This night is called Shab-e-Maraj.

And especially found in humans only. For example, a throne for Allah to sit on is his hands, he also has eyes. His life is also mentioned in the Qur'an. Muslim scholars are silent on commenting on some of these qualities, ending the discussion by saying only that we should accept these qualities of Allah as mentioned in the Qur'an without doubt and should not make them a matter of debate. needed . Some scholars, especially those who follow the Motazilah school of thought, have refused to accept these qualities such as seeing, hearing, speaking etc., because these qualities require a body and Allah is not corporeal. These thinkers have written while explaining the 'hand of Allah' that it is not a physical part, but it means that Allah is powerful or He is very kind. Instead of taking the literal meaning of such words, we should take the meaning.

(iv) **The Creator --**

This creation is the creation of Allah. The actions of Allah can be estimated by considering this creation. Nature and all the objects of nature have been called signs (imports). By looking at these signs, our attention goes to the Creator. Islamic philosophy does not believe in causality and believes in the belief that there was no world in the beginning. It came into existence by the order of Allah. Does the creation fulfill any of Allah's goals? In answer to this, Muslim scholars think that Allah created this universe to reveal his power and follow-up. It is mentioned in a hadith that Allah was an invisible treasure. He wanted creation to happen and it happened. This concept is similar in many respects to the Jewish concept of God found in the Old Testament. But the concept of God that we find in the New Testament (Injil) is different from the Islamic concept in that there is no distance or gulf between man and God. God reveals his form to man in his immense love, whereas according to Islamic belief, Allah remains a master, a master, and man remains a servant of this master. Man cannot rise above the status of a servant. No matter how close a man is to his Allah, and no matter how close Allah is to his servant, he can neither know nor understand Allah. There is only master-servant relationship in Islam, there is a sense of praise in favor of the servant, not a sense of friend.

Reference- An Introduction to Islam, Author-Sam.Wahin.Bhajan, Benjamin Khan.

history of the word allah

Regional versions of the word dharma Allah in pre-Islamic Arabia are found in both pagan and Christian pre-Islamic inscriptions. Various theories have been proposed regarding the role of Allah in pre-Islamic polytheistic cults. According to the Islamic scholar Ibn Kathir, Arab pagans regarded Allah as an invisible god who created and controlled the universe. Pagans believed that worshiping humans or animals who had lucky events in their lives brought them closer to God. The pre-Islamic Meccans worshiped Allah along with a host of lesser deities and whom they called "daughters of Allah".

Islam forbade worshiping anything other than God. Some authors have suggested that the polytheistic Arabs used this name to refer to a creator god or the supreme deity of their pantheon. The term may be ambiguous in Meccan religion.

According to one hypothesis, which goes back to Julius Wellhausen, Allah (supreme deity of the tribal confederacy surrounding the Quraysh) was a designation that distinguished the superiority of Hubal (supreme deity of the Quraysh) over other deities. However, there is also evidence that Allah and Hubal were two different gods. According to that hypothesis, the Kaaba It was first revered as a supreme deity named Allah and then hosted the shrine of the

Quraysh after their conquest of Mecca, about a century before Muhammad's time. Some inscriptions seem to indicate the use of Allah as the name of a polytheistic deity centuries earlier, but nothing is known precisely about this use. Some scholars have suggested that Allah may represent a distant creator god who was gradually eclipsed by more specific local deities. There is disagreement as to whether Allah played a prominent role in the Meccan religious pantheon. No iconic representation of Allah exists. Allah is the only deity in Mecca who does not have an idol. Muhammad's father's name was 'Abd-Allah which means "servant of Allah".

1
2
3
4
5
6
7

Arabic components forming the word "Allah":

1-Alif

2-Hamzat Wal (همزة وصل)

3-lam

4-lam

5-Shadda (शद्दा)

6-Dagger Alif (ألف خنجرية)

7- Yes

The etymology of the word Allah has been widely discussed by classical Arab linguists. Grammarists of the Basra school regard it either as "naturally" (murtajal) or as a definite form of lah (from the oral root lih with the meaning of "elevated" or "hidden"). Others held that it was borrowed from Syriac or Hebrew, but most commonly attribute it to a contraction of the Arabic definite articles al- "the" and ilāh "god, lord" from al-lah meaning "god", or Most modern scholars support the latter theory, and view the Loanward hypothesis with skepticism.

Cognate words for the name "Allah" exist in other Semitic languages, including Hebrew and Aramaic. The corresponding Aramaic form is Elah (אלה), but its emphatic state is Elaha (אלהא). It is written in Biblical Aramaic as ܐܠܗܐ ('Ĕlāhā) and in Syriac as ܐܲܠܵܗܵܐ ('Alâhâ), both of which simply mean "Lord".

Allah (listen)) is the generic Arabic word for God. In the English language, the term generally refers to God in Islam. The word is believed to be derived by contraction from al-ilāh, meaning "god", and linguistically from the Aramaic word ela and the Syriac ܐܲܠܵܗܵܐ ('Alāhā). And the Hebrew word El (Elohim) is related to God. The female form of Allah is considered to be the word Allat.

The word 'Allah' in Arabic calligraphy

The word Allah has been used by Arabic people of various religions since pre-Islamic times. Pre-Islamic Arabs worshiped a supreme deity they called Allah along with other minor deities. Muhammad used the word Allah to denote the Islamic concept of God. Allah has been used as a term for God by Muslims (both Arabs and non-Arabs) and even Arab Christians, followed by the words "al-Illah" and "Allah" by the majority of Arabs. was used interchangeably in classical Arabic. had become Muslims. It is often, though not exclusively, used in this way by Bábists, Bahá'ís, Mandaeans, Indonesian and Maltese Christians, and Sephardi Jews, as well as the Gagauz people. Similar use by Christians and Sikhs in West Malaysia has recently given rise to political and legal controversies.

Although the two statements of the shahada are present in the Qur'an (for example, 37:35 and 48:29), they are not found side by side as in the shahada sutras, but are present in the hadiths. Versions of both phrases began to appear on coins and monumental architecture in the late seventh century, which suggests that it was not officially established as a ritual statement of faith until then. An inscription in the Dome of the Rock (est. 692) in Jerusalem reads: "There is no god but God alone; He has no partner with Him; Muhammad is the Messenger of God". Another version appears in coins minted after the reign of the fifth Umayyad caliph, Abd al-Malik ibn Marwan: "Muhammad is God's servant and his messenger". Although it is unclear when the shahada first came into common use among Muslims, it is clear that the sentiments it expresses were part of the Qur'an and Islamic doctrine from early times.

The use of the word Allah in the national flag of an Islamic country

Under Soviet rule, the Union Republic – now located in modern-day Uzbekistan – used a flag derived from the flag of the Soviet Union and representing communism, approved in 1952. The flag is similar to the Soviet design but with a blue stripe 1/5 the width and two 1/100 white edging in the middle.

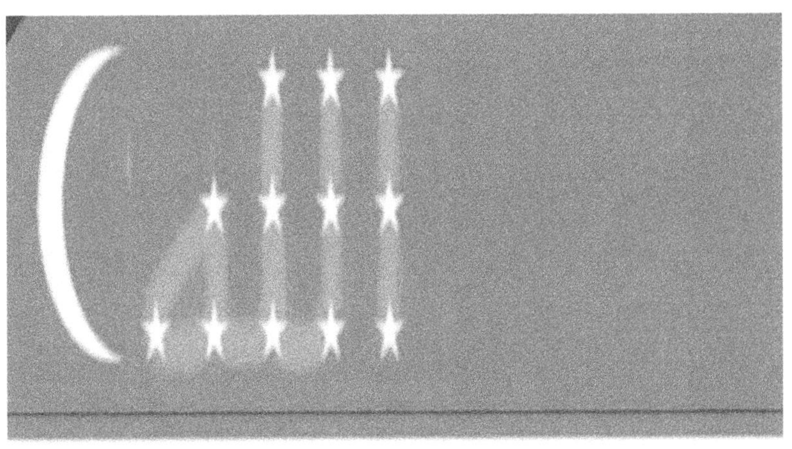

Uzbekistan declared itself independent on 1 September 1991, about three months before the dissolution of the Soviet Union. Soon after, the search for a national flag began, with a competition being held to determine a new design. More than 200 submissions were made, and a commission was formed to evaluate these suggestions coming from various stakeholders. The winning design was adopted on 18 November 1991, after being chosen at an extraordinary session of the Uzbek Supreme Soviet. In doing so, Uzbekistan became the first independent republic in Central Asia to choose a new flag. With respect to its tricolor combination of blue, white and green horizontal stripes, it is similar to the flags of Lesotho, an annexed country bordering South Africa, and Puntland, a Somali federal state at the tip of the Horn.

الله أكبر

'Allahu Akbaru' (أَكْبَرُ اللهُ), meaning "God is the greatest".

It is a common Arabic expression, used by Muslims and Arabs around the world in a variety of contexts: in formal Salah (prayer), in Adhan (call to Islamic prayer), in Hajj, as an informal expression of faith, In times of distress or happiness, or to express determination or defiance. The phrase is also used by Arab Christians.

Christianity

Today's Christian Arabs have no other word for "God" than "Allah." Similarly, the Aramaic word for "God" in the language of Assyrian Christians is 'ĕlāhā, or 'Alāhā. (Even the Arabic-origin Maltese language of Malta, whose population is almost entirely Catholic, uses Allāh for "God.")

Arab Christians have used two forms of invocation that were fused at the beginning of their written works. They adopted the Muslim Bismillah, and also created their own Trinitarian Bismillah in the early 8th century. The Muslim Bismillah reads: "In the name of God, the Compassionate, the Merciful." The Trinitarian Bismillah reads: "In the name of the Father and the Son and the Holy Spirit, one God." The Syriac, Latin, and Greek invocations do not have the words "one God" at the end. This addition was made to emphasize the monotheistic aspect of the trinitarian faith and to make it more acceptable to Muslims.

Sufism

In Tasawwuf, often described as the inner, mystical dimension of Islam, Hu, Huwa (depending on the place in the sentence), or Parvardigar in Persian is used as the name of God. The Hu sound is derived from the last letter of the word Allah, which is read as Allahu in the middle of a sentence. Hu means 'the Just One' or 'the Manifested'. The word appears clearly in several verses of the Quran: La ilaha illa hu"

—Al-Imran:18

God in the Bahá'í Faith

The scriptures of the Bahá'í Faith often refer to God by various titles and attributes, such as Almighty, All-Powerful, All-Powerful, All-Wise, Incomparable, Merciful, Helpful, All-Glorious, and Omniscient. Bahá'ís believe that the greatest name of God is "the All-Glorious", or Bahá in Arabic. Bahá'í is the root word of the following names and phrases: the greeting Alláh-u-Abhá ('God is All-Glorious'), the invocation or Bahá'u'lláh ('Glory to the Most Glorious'), Bahá'u'lláh ('Glory to God'), and Bahá'í ('Follower of the All-Glorious'). These are expressed in Arabic, regardless of the language used (see Bahá'í symbols). In addition to these names, God is also addressed in local languages, for example Ishwar in Hindi, Dieu in French, and Dios in Spanish. Bahá'ís believe that Bahá'u'lláh, the founder of the Bahá'í Faith, is "the perfect embodiment of the names and attributes of God".

Mandaeanism

The Mandaeans believe in one God called Hayi Rabbi ('Great Life' or 'Great Living God'). Other names used for God include Mare d'Rabuta ('Lord of Greatness'), Mana Rabba ('Great Mind'), Melka d'Nhura ('King of Light') and Hayi Qadmai ('First Life').

Yazidi Religion

The Yazidi religion knows only one eternal God, often named Zwedde. According to some Yazidi hymns (known as Qewls), God has 1001 names.

101 Names of God in Zoroastrianism

In Zoroastrianism, the 101 Names of God (Pazand Sad-o-Yak Nam-i-Khoda) is a list of the names of God (Ahura Mazda). This list is preserved in Persian, Pazand, and Gujarati. The Zoroastrian tradition expanded it to a list of 101 names of God.

Mu'tazilis

Mu'tazilis reject anthropomorphic attributes of God because an eternal being "must be unique" and attributes make God comparable. The descriptions of God in the Quran are considered metaphorical. Nevertheless, Mu'tazilis believed that God has unity (tawhid) and justice. Other attributes, such as wisdom, are not ascribed to God; rather they describe his essence. Otherwise God's eternal attributes would give rise to a multitude of eternally existing entities besides God.

Among the most important Mu'tazili theological works are:

Sharh al-Usul al-Khamsa (Explanation of the Five Principles) by al-Qadi 'Abd al-Jabbar (died 415/1025).

al-Minhaj fi Usul al-Din (Course/Method in the Fundamentals of Religion) by al-Zamakhshari (died 538/1144).

Shi'ites

The Shi'ites agreed with the Mu'tazilites and denied that God would be seen with physical eyes in this world or in the next.

Ismailis

According to Ismailism, God is absolutely transcendental and unknowable; beyond matter, energy, space, time, change, imagination, intellect, positive and negative qualities. All the attributes of God named in rituals, scriptures or prayers refer not to qualities that God possesses, but to qualities that emanate from God, thus these are qualities that God has given as the source of all qualities, but God is not based on any of these qualities. A philosophical definition of Allah of the world is "the being who concentrates in himself all the attributes of perfection" or "the being who is the essential being, and who contains all the attributes of perfection". Since God is beyond all words, Ismailism also denies the concept of God as the first cause.

In Ismailism, assigning attributes to God as well as denying any of God's attributes (via negation) both qualify as anthropomorphism and are rejected, since God can be understood neither by assigning attributes to Him nor by removing attributes from Him. The 10th-century Ismaili philosopher Abu Ya'qub al-Sijistani suggested the method of double negation; for example: "God does not exist" is followed by "God is not non-existent". This glorifies God beyond any understanding or human comprehension.

Twelver

Theology of Twelvers

Twelver Shi'ites believe that God has no shape, no physical hands, no physical feet, no physical body, no physical face. They believe that God has no visible form. God does not change with time, nor does He inhabit any physical location. Shi'ites argue that God does not change under any circumstances. There is also no time limit regarding God. In support of their view, Shi'ite scholars often cite the Quranic verse 6:103 which states: "Eyes do not comprehend Him, but He comprehends all eyes. He is Omniscient (all-perceptive, no matter how small), Omniscient." Thus a fundamental difference between Sunnis and Shi'ites is that the former believe that followers will "see" their God on the Day of Resurrection, while the latter believe that God cannot be seen because He is beyond space and time.

Ibn Abbas says that once a Bedouin came to Allah's Messenger and said, "Allah's Messenger! Teach me the most unusual knowledge!" He asked him, "What have you done with the summit of knowledge that you now ask about its most unusual things?" The man asked him, "Allah's Messenger! What is this summit of knowledge?" He said, "It is knowing Allah in the way He should be known." Then the Bedouin said, "And how can He be known in the way He should be known?" Allah's Messenger replied, "It is that you know Him that

He has no ideal, no counterpart, no adversary, and that He is Wahid (one, single) and Ahad (unique, absolutely one): Apparent yet Hidden, the First and the Last, having no counterpart or likeness; this is the true knowledge of Him."

—Muhammad Baqir al-Majlisi, "Knowing Allah", Bihar al-Anwar

Among the most important Shia theological works are:

Kitab al-Tawhid (Book of Monotheism) by Ibn Babawayh – also known as al-Shaykh al-Saduq – (d. 381 H/991).

Tajrid al-Itqidah (Sublimation of Faith) by Nasir al-Din al-Tusi (d. 672/1274).

As a loanword

English and other European languages

The history of the name Allāh in English was probably influenced by the study of comparative religion in the 19th century; for example, Thomas Carlyle (1840) sometimes used the term Allah but without any implication that Allah was anything different from God. However, in his biography of Muḥammad (1934), Tor Andræ always used the term Allah, though he allows that this "conception of God" seems to imply that it is different from that of the Jewish and Christian theologies.

Languages which may not commonly use the term Allah to denote God may still contain popular expressions which use the word. For example, because of the centuries long Muslim presence in the Iberian Peninsula, the word ojalá in the Spanish language and oxalá in the Portuguese language exist today, borrowed from Andalusi Arabic law šá lláh similar to inshalla . This phrase literally means 'if God wills' (in the sense of "I hope so"). The German poet Mahlmann used the form "Allah" as the title of a poem about the ultimate deity, though it is unclear how much Islamic thought he intended to convey.

Some Muslims leave the name "Allāh" untranslated in English, rather than using the English translation "God". The word has also been applied to certain living human beings as personifications of the term and concept.

Malaysian and Indonesian language
Titular Roman Catholic Archbishop of Kuala Lumpur v. Menteri Dalam Negeri and 2010 attacks against places of worship in Malaysia

The first dictionary of Dutch-Malay by A.C. Ruyl, Justus Heurnius, and Caspar Wiltens in 1650 recorded Allah as the translation of the Dutch word Godt.

Gereja Kalam Kebangunan Allah (Word of God Revival Church) in Indonesia. Allah is the word for "God" in the Indonesian language - even in Alkitab (Christian Bible, from الكتاب al-kitāb = the book) translations, while Tuhan is the word for "Lord".

Christians in Malaysia and Indonesia use Allah to refer to God in the Malaysian and Indonesian languages (both of them standardized forms of the Malay language). Mainstream Bible translations in the language use Allah as the translation of Hebrew Elohim (translated in English Bibles as "God"). This goes back to early translation work by Francis Xavier in the 16th century. The first dictionary of Dutch-Malay by Albert Cornelius Ruyl, Justus Heurnius, and Caspar Wiltens in 1650 (revised edition from 1623 edition and 1631 Latin edition) recorded Allah" as the translation of the Dutch word Godt. Ruyl also translated the Gospel of Matthew in 1612 into the

Malay language (an early Bible translation into a non-European language, made a year after the publication of the King James Version), which was printed in the Netherlands in 1629. Then he translated the Gospel of Mark, published in 1638.

The government of Malaysia in 2007 outlawed usage of the term Allah in any other but Muslim contexts, but the Malayan High Court in 2009 revoked the law, ruling it unconstitutional. While Allah had been used for the Christian God in Malay for more than four centuries, the contemporary controversy was triggered by usage of Allah by the Roman Catholic newspaper The Herald. The government appealed the court ruling, and the High Court suspended implementation of its verdict until the hearing of the appeal. In October 2013 the court ruled in favor of the government's ban. In early 2014 the Malaysian government confiscated more than 300 bibles for using the word to refer to the Christian God in Peninsular Malaysia. However, the use of Allah is not prohibited in the two Malaysian states of Sabah and Sarawak. The main reason it is not prohibited in these two states is that usage has been long-established and local Alkitab (Bibles) have been widely distributed freely in East Malaysia without restrictions for years. Both states also do not have similar Islamic state laws as those in West Malaysia.

In reaction to some media criticism, the Malaysian government has introduced a "10-point solution" to avoid confusion and misleading information. The 10-point solution is in line with the spirit of the 18- and 20-point agreements of Sarawak and Sabah.

The postulation that Allah (God in Islam) originated as a moon god first arose in 1901 in the scholarship of archaeologist Hugo Winckler. He identified Allah with a pre-Islamic Arabian deity known as Lah or Hubal, which he called a lunar deity. This notion has been dismissed by modern scholarship as being without basis.

A similar notion was propagated in the United States in the 1990s by Christian apologists using a 1994 pamphlet The Moon-god Allah: In Archeology of the Middle East by the Christian pastor Robert Morey. This was followed by the 2001 book by Morey called The Islamic Invasion: Confronting the World's Fastest-Growing Religion. Morey argued that "Allah" was a moon goddess in pre-Islamic Arabic mythology, and pointed to Islam's use of a lunar calendar and the use of moon imagery in Islam as support.

Modern scholars have dismissed the original theory and its popularized form as unevidenced. The whole notion is considered speculative and without basis in the archaeological record of the development of religion on the Arabian peninsula. It has also been labelled an insult both to Muslims and to Arab Christians, as the latter also refers to God as "Allah".

Before Islam, the Kaaba contained a statue representing the god Hubal. On the basis that the Kaaba was also Allah's house, Julius Wellhausen considered Hubal to be an ancient name for Allah. The 20th-century scholar Hugo Winckler in turn claimed that Hubal was a moon god, though others have suggested otherwise. David Leeming describes him as a warrior and rain god, as does Mircea Eliade.

More recent scholars have rejected this view, partly because it is speculation but also because of the Nabataean origins of Hubal, a non-native deity imported into the Southern Arabian shrine – one which may have already been associated with Allah. Patricia Crone argues that "If Hubal and Allah had been one and the same deity, Hubal ought to have survived as an epithet of Allah, which he did not. And moreover there would not have been traditions in which people are asked to renounce the one for the other." Joseph Lumbard, a professor of classical Islam, has stated that the idea is "not only an insult to Muslims but also an insult to Arab Christians who use the name 'Allah' for God."

Christian proponents

Pat Robertson promoted the idea

Robert Morey's book The Moon-god Allah in the Archeology of the Middle East claims that Al-'Uzzá is identical in origin to Hubal, whom he asserts to be a lunar deity. This teaching is repeated in the Chick tracts "Allah Had No Son" and "The Little Bride". In 1996 Janet Parshall, in syndicated radio broadcasts, asserted that Muslims worship a moon god. Pat Robertson said in 2003, "The struggle is whether Hubal, the Moon God of Mecca, known as Allah, is supreme, or whether the Judeo-Christian Jehovah God of the Bible is Supreme."

However, recent research from various sources has proven that the "evidence" used by Morey was of the statue retrieved from an excavation site at Hazor, of which there is no connection to "Allah" at all. In fact, Bible scholar and mission strategist Rick Brown openly disagrees with this approach and said:

Those who claim that Allah is a pagan deity, most notably the moon god, often base their claims on the fact that a symbol of the crescent moon adorns the tops of many mosques and is widely used as a symbol of Islam. It is in fact true that before the coming of Islam many "gods" and idols were worshipped in the Middle East, but the name of the moon god was Sîn, not Allah, and he was not particularly popular in Arabia, the birthplace of Islam. The most prominent idol in Mecca was a god called Hubal, and there is no proof that he was a moon god. It is sometimes claimed that there is a temple to the moon god at Hazor in Palestine. This is based on a representation there of a supplicant wearing a crescent-like pendant. It is not clear, however, that the pendant symbolizes a moon god, and in any case this is not an Arab religious site but an ancient Canaanite site, which was destroyed by Joshua in about 1250 BC. ... If the ancient Arabs worshipped hundreds of idols, then no doubt the moon god Sîn was included, for even the Hebrews were prone to worship the sun and the moon and the stars, but there is no clear evidence that moon-worship was prominent among the Arabs in any way or that the crescent was used as the symbol of a moon god, and Allah was certainly not the moon god's name.

In 2009, anthropologist Gregory Starrett wrote, "a recent survey by the Council for American Islamic Relations reports that as many as 10% of Americans believe Muslims are pagans who worship a moon god or goddess, a belief energetically disseminated by some Christian activists." Ibrahim Hooper of the Council on American-Islamic Relations (CAIR) calls the Moon-God theories of Allah evangelical "fantasies" that are "perpetuated in their comic books".

Farzana Hassan sees these views as an extension of long-standing Christian claims that Muhammad was an impostor and deceiver, and has stated: "Literature circulated by the Christian Coalition perpetuates the popular Christian belief about Islam being a pagan religion, borrowing aspects of Judeo-Christian monotheism by elevating the moon god Hubal to the rank of Supreme God, or Allah. Muhammad, for fundamentalist Christians, remains an impostor who commissioned his companions to copy words of the Bible as they sat in dark inaccessible places, far removed from public gaze."

Muslim views

In 8th-century Arab historian Hisham Ibn Al-Kalbi's Book of Idols, the idol Hubal is described as a human figure with a gold hand (replacing the original hand that had broken off the statue). He had seven arrows that were used for divination.

Whether or not Hubal was even associated with the moon, Muhammad and his enemies identified Hubal and Allah as different gods, their supporters fighting on opposing sides in the Battle of Uhud. Ibn Hisham notes that Abu Sufyan ibn Harb, leader of the anti-Islamic army, glorified Hubal after their perceived victory at Uhud:

When Abū Sufyān wanted to leave he went to the top of the mountain and shouted loudly saying, 'You have done a fine work; victory in war goes by turns. Today in exchange for the day (T. of Badr). Show your superiority, Hubal,' i.c. vindicate your religion. The apostle told 'Umar to get up and answer him and say, 'God is most high and most glorious. We are not equal. Our dead are in paradise; your dead in hell.'

The Quran itself forbids moon worship in verse 37 of Surah Fussilat:

"Do not prostrate to the sun or to the moon, but prostrate to Allah, who created them."

Islam teaches that Allah is the name of God (as iterated in the Quran), and is the same god worshipped by the members of other Abrahamic religions such as Christianity and Judaism (Quran 29:46).

Pre-Islamic traditions

Before Muhammad, Allah was not considered the sole divinity by the Meccans; however, Allah was considered the creator of the world and the giver of rain. The notion of the term may have been vague in the Meccan religion. Allah was associated with companions, whom pre-Islamic Arabs considered as subordinate deities. Meccans held that a kind of kinship existed between Allah and the jinn. Allah have had sons and daughters. The Meccans possibly associated angels with Allah. Allah was invoked in times of distress.

Muhammad's father's name was عبد الله ʿAbd-Allāh meaning 'the slave of Allāh'.

Al-Ism al-Aʿẓam

Al-Ism al-Aʿẓam literally "the Greatest Name", also known as Ism Allah al-Akbar (اسم الله الأكبر, 'the Greatest Name of God'), refers in Islam to the greatest name of Allah, known only to the prophets.

Significance

According to some Islamic hadiths, whoever calls to God using al-Ism al-A'zam, his or her prayer (du'a) will be granted.

In Shi'a Islam, al-Ism al-A'zam is believed to have a powerful effect in the act of blessing.

Judaism

Elah

Elah (אֱלָה, pl. Elim or Elohim; Imperial Aramaic: אלהא) is the Aramaic word for God and the absolute singular form of אלהא, 'ilāhā. The origin of the word is from Proto-Semitic ʔil and is thus cognate to the Hebrew, Arabic, Akkadian, and other Semitic languages' words for god. Elah is found in the Tanakh in the books of Ezra, Jeremiah (Jeremiah 10:11, the only verse in the entire book written in Aramaic), and Daniel. Elah is used to describe both pagan gods and the Abrahamic God.

Elah Yisrael, God of Israel (Ezra 5:1)
Elah Yerushelem, God of Jerusalem (Ezra 7:19)
Elah Shemaya, God of Heaven (Ezra 7:23)
Elah-avahati, God of my fathers, (Daniel 2:23)
Elah Elahin, God of gods (Daniel 2:47)

El Roi

In the Book of Genesis, Hagar uses this name for the God who spoke to her through his angel. In Hebrew, her phrase El Roi, literally, 'God of Seeing Me', is translated in the King James Version as "Thou God seest me."

Elyon

The name Elyon (עליון) occurs in combination with El, YHWH, Elohim and alone. It appears chiefly in poetic and later Biblical passages. The modern Hebrew adjective 'Elyon means 'supreme' (as in "Supreme Court": Hebrew: בית המשפט העליון) or 'Most High'. El Elyon has been traditionally translated into English as 'God Most High'. The Phoenicians used what appears to be a similar name for God, one that the Greeks wrote as Ἐλιονα.

My another books

Sr no.	Book
1	World's Major religions, doctrines and sects
2	An introduction to the Holy Qur'an and it's unsolved mysteries
3	How did humans and language originate ?
4	Islam an introduction and sect
5	Sermons of great people
6	Prayer
7	Allah an introduction
8	Is Al khizr still alive today?
9	Story of harut and marut
10	Grief
11	The mysterious story of Al kahf (Ar raqim)
12	Naming of God
13	Who was Sheeba?
14	Death concept of the Holy Quran

15	What is soul? In view of Religion and science
16	Real Alexander Zulqurnain
17	Where is peace?
18	Origin of ancient religious book, it's author and original copy
19	An introduction to the bible and is the original bible still available today?
20	Does a parallel universe exist?
21	Promise to your self or God?
22	Evidence of God existance
23	Prediction of holy Quran
24	Humanity in the holy Quran?
25	Commandnends of the holy Quran,right or wrong?
26	Similarity in the world famous holy books
27	Is Zulkifl the same Gautam Buddha?
28	Adam to Muhammad
29	Why isolated?

30	For Divorce! Who is responsible?
31	Hadith to denomination
32	Karma is the best?
33	According to dreams, religion and Science
34	End day

<u>All these books are available in Hindi</u> language and other international languages and are also available in e-book for <u>free on Google Play Store</u>.

<u>All the books are available in paper back edition and hard cover edition as well.</u>

<u>These books are also available on Amazon,Flipkart and notionpress.com.</u>

My personal introduction

My name is Abdul Waheed, my father's name is Late Haji Ubaidur Rahman and mother's name is Jaibunnisa. I have liked scientific ideology since childhood and have a calm nature and attachment to books. Due to which my curiosity interest has been continuously used in new discoveries and information. I got selected in polytechnic while doing BSc, but unfortunately it remained incomplete because father and brother died. Two words of my father, which are very precious for my life, first - earn honestly, do not take support of lies, secondly, respect food and eat as much as you want. That's why the education remained incomplete due to the responsibility of the house, then later getting married. Still did not lose courage and today the book is available in front of you in the form of my thoughts. If any information is left incomplete, please let us know.

Thank you .

www.ingramcontent.com/pod-product-compliance
Lightning Source LLC
Chambersburg PA
CBHW040130150726
48005CB00015B/2436